A Soldier's Life

in the

CIVIL WAR

Peter F. Copeland

DOVER PUBLICATIONS, INC.
Mineola, New York

Bibliographical Note

A Soldier's Life in the Civil War is a new work, first published by Dover Publications, Inc., in 2001.

DOVER *Pictorial Archive* SERIES

This book belongs to the Dover Pictorial Archive Series. You may use the designs and illustrations for graphics and crafts applications, free and without special permission, provided that you include no more than four in the same publication or project. (For permission for additional use, please write to Permissions Department, Dover Publications, Inc., 31 East 2nd Street, Mineola, N.Y. 11501.)

However, republication or reproduction of any illustration by any other graphic service, whether it be in a book or in any other design resource, is strictly prohibited.

International Standard Book Number: 0-486-41544-9

Manufactured in the United States of America
Dover Publications, Inc., 31 East 2nd Street, Mineola, N.Y. 11501

Introduction

The ordinary life of a soldier is often obscured by the dramatic images of victories and defeats in battle. But what was a soldier's day-to-day life during the Civil War really like? Camp life was characterized by routines. Reveille was sounded at 5 a.m. during the summer and at 6 a.m. during the winter. After roll call, the soldiers put the camp in order and ate breakfast. Their daily routine included as many as five drill sessions, conducted, in the early days of the war, by officers whose skills were as rudimentary as those of the recruits. Dress parade and inspection in late afternoon were followed by supper around 6:30 p.m. Soldiers not on picket (sentry) duty were free for the rest of the evening. "Lights out" took place at 9:00 p.m. During the winter, when drills were curtailed by severe weather, soldiers passed the time by playing cards, chess, reading, and telling stories. Musical performances, both impromptu and scheduled, also provided entertainment. Men sang sentimental songs around the campfire to express—and ease—their homesickness.

There is a general awareness of the difficulties of life in the trenches, but less familiarity with the miseries and deprivations of life in a military encampment. The excitement and enthusiasm of many new recruits waned as they repeated drill after drill at camp and choked on the thick dust raised while marching. Spoiled, vermin-infested rations and filthy camp conditions were dispiriting and caused illness as well. Soldiers who broke the rules were subjected to humiliating punishments. Yet the recruits had many opportunities for friendship and comradeship during the war. And when Johnny Reb and Billy Yank—the representative soldiers of the South and North—made contact during peaceful interludes, they were often surprised to find how much they had in common.

Being wounded or taken ill during the Civil War was cause for dread. Many more soldiers died from infectious diseases and negligent medical care than were killed in battle. Civil War doctors and surgeons were largely ignorant of contemporary medical advances in other parts of the world, and their ignorance led to prolonged agony and death for many men. For example, surgeons unknowingly spread infection by using unsterilized equipment and by using their bare hands when treating wounds.

The plight of prisoners of war was also severe. Three thousand inadequately clothed, emaciated Confederate soldiers died in the prison camp at Elmira, New York; 13,000 Union men died in less than a year at Andersonville, Georgia, chiefly from a lack of medical care.

When the war ended in 1865, those who had participated headed home to resume their lives. For many veterans, however, it was hard to settle down to a normal life after the challenges, demands, and excitement of the war. Those who could settle down did so, but many others began a restless search for a new life.

Volunteers at a Recruiting Office

The majority of soldiers engaged in the Civil War were volunteers. Recruiting offices were hastily set up; those who signed up for service took an oath of allegiance and were then sent to a nearby camp for outfitting and training. Here we see a typical recruiting office opened early in the war. In the foreground, a recently recruited, uniformed volunteer regales a young friend with tales of army life and adventures in camp.

New Recruits Receiving Clothing and Equipment

Upon arriving at camp, recruits were given a hasty physical examination and were formally mustered into service. The Articles of War were read and recruits were issued uniform clothing and equipment. Men often received garments too large or small for them and traded with other recruits until they found a proper fit. Uniform clothing, shoes, socks, underwear, overcoat, canteen, haversack, knapsack, belts, cartridge box, bayonet, and musket were among the items issued under the watchful eye of the quartermaster sergeant, shown at the rear.

A Farewell to Loved Ones

For the young volunteer fortunate enough to be recruited close to home, the day came when marching orders were received and he was able to get a pass to say good-bye to his loved ones. Shown here is a young soldier in full equipment bidding farewell to his childhood sweetheart as his anxious parents look on.

Learning the Musketry Drill

The young recruit had to quickly adjust to a regimental routine that differed greatly from civilian life. Bugle calls and drums regulated the soldier's day. Here we see the "awkward squad"—those men not yet adept at musketry drill—being punished by having to repeat the commands in the hot sun while their comrades looked on.

Reveille at Daybreak

At 5 a.m. the camp was roused by reveille, performed by bugle and drums, summoning men to roll call. A brief drill and breakfast followed. The bugle sounded sick call after breakfast, and fatigue duties such as cleaning quarters, policing the campgrounds, and cutting wood for camp and cooking fires were performed.

Learning to Use the Musket

Here we see the young recruits being instructed in the use and care of the musket. The weapon was usually a .58 caliber muzzle-loading single-shot Springfield or Enfield rifled musket fitted with a spike bayonet, accurate at ranges of from 200 to 300 yards. A number of soldiers received breech-loading repeating rifles, and cavalrymen carried short-barreled carbines. The sergeant shown above is instructing the men on the loading procedure: after the charge (a cartridge containing powder and ball) is rammed down the barrel, a percussion cap is fitted to the nipple, which, when struck by the hammer, explodes the charge.

Inspection on the Parade Ground

At about 8 a.m., each company was called up for inspection by the first sergeant and then marched out to the regimental parade ground. In the afternoon, before dress parade, there was an inspection by the company commander, as we see here. The men were inspected for personal appearance and correctness of uniform, equipment, and weapons; they were expected to keep their muskets clean and in good working order. These men are using ram-rods to ensure that no old charges remained in the musket barrels.

Free Time After the Last Roll Call

The soldier's day in camp ended after dress parade and supper, when the bugle sounded the tattoo—marking the last roll call and time for men to go to their quarters—followed by taps, the last bugle call, signaling "lights out." Here we see a scene in summer camp after evening supper, when the men cleaned up, straightened their gear, cleaned their shoes and muskets, and relaxed, perhaps playing a hand of cards, singing, or telling tales.

A Soldier at the Camp Infirmary

During the Civil War, more soldiers died of illnesses such as "camp fever" than were killed or wounded on the battlefield. Many men, especially those from isolated rural areas, died in alarming numbers from diseases such as measles, mumps, chicken pox, and scarlet fever. Medical science was in its infancy and there were few competent doctors—American doctors lagged behind their European colleagues in understanding how illness was spread. This trainee has collapsed during a drill and will be treated in the camp infirmary.

Writing a Letter Home

When not involved in drill, standing guard, or performing other duties, soldiers used their spare time for activities such as reading, playing cards, or writing letters. Here, a homesick soldier writes to his parents; his comrades play cards.

Officers' Wives on a Camp Visit

It was a gala occasion when the colonel's lady, accompanied perhaps by wives of other officers, visited the camp. All turned out to see them, and there was usually a band concert in their honor.

The visits ordinarily took place over the weekend. Compared to the officers' wives, soldiers' wives did not often have the means or opportunity for such visits.

On Sentry Duty

Sentry duty was a regular part of the soldier's duties. Sentries were posted in all weather around the camp and were regularly relieved every few hours. This young soldier is on quarter guard, doing sentry duty in the area of the company's tents.

Caring for a Minor Injury

When they were not marching, soldiers kept busy on details such as building roads, digging latrines, and cutting wood. The lucky young soldier shown here was able to evade these duties by reporting a minor injury and having it cared for by a nurse at the hospital tent during sick call.

The Pleasures of Music at Camp

Playing music and singing were popular diversions of camp life, shown here in an impromptu gathering where the fiddler performs a popular tune on an instrument fashioned from a cigar box. Soldiers sang ballads such as "Home Sweet Home" while gathered around the campfire. In addition, the regimental bands offered more formal concerts.

A Hungry Soldier Finds Food

The soldiers of both armies learned that when in the field it was often necessary to supplement army rations with corn, potatoes, berries from a farmer's field, or whatever else they could find. When the cook's wagon failed to keep up with the troops on campaign it was sometimes every man for himself. In addition, many officers were unable to pay for their meals when their wages were late. Here we see a hungry young volunteer in a cornfield.

The Diversion of a Card Game

Whenever there were soldiers in camp there were card games. Gambling was a favorite pastime, even when forbidden by local commanders. In the face of battle, the decks of cards came out, and men risked what little they had on a turn of the card while waiting orders to advance.

A Visit from the Photographer

Photographers worked in cities and towns, some of which were located near military bases, and they did a thriving business photographing soldiers during the war years. Each man wanted a picture of himself in uniform to send home to his family. Here a young soldier in full dress uniform, his head held steady by a brace, stares belligerently into the lens while his comrades look on.

The Eagerly Awaited Mail Wagon

Perhaps the most eagerly awaited event in camp was mail call. A word from loved ones might cheer a homesick soldier. The mail was delivered in camp and in the field during campaigns wherever possible. The army mail wagons traveled with the troops, sometimes even on the eve of battle.

Enjoying the Sutler's Wares

The sutler's tent sold many items that were not included in the army's supplies, such as tobacco, clothing, canned meats, newspapers, candy, and fried pies. The sutler was a licensed traveling salesman who followed the Army in his wagon. Many soldiers resented the overcharging but were eager nonetheless to make their purchases. Here we see some young volunteers whose liquid refreshment is about to be confiscated by an alert officer.

Trade Between Blue and Gray

Throughout the war, soldiers on both sides often engaged in trading. Wherever the opposing armies lay near each other, pickets, or advance guards of the two forces, sometimes contacted each other to swap items that were in short supply. Confederates often swapped tobacco, which they frequently had plenty of, for coffee, tea, or other such items which, thanks to northern maritime commerce, the Yankees possessed.

A Humiliating Punishment

Both northern and southern armies resorted to a variety of punishments to maintain discipline. A common punishment for minor offenses was for the offender to be chained to a 32-lb. cannonball and forced to walk through camp, dragging the ball behind him. Two offenders, seen here, wear the "wooden overcoat" or "barrel shirt," fitted out with a sign announcing their offense. Under guard, the miscreants were marched around camp, subjected to contempt and ridicule. Other punishments included digging trenches, cleaning latrines, and extra guard duty.

Finding Solace in Religion

Religion played a significant part in the lives of soldiers, both north and south, and officers on both sides depended upon religion and the work of the army chaplains to promote order and decency in the soldiers' lives and behavior. Volunteers from the U.S. Christian Commission, as we see here, distributed bibles and hymn books, held prayer meetings, and offered lonely and troubled soldiers free coffee and counseling.

Receiving Military Rations

Soldiers were more or less adequately fed while in camp. Men on both sides went hungry at times when the Commissary wagons could not keep up with the rapidly moving troops. In the field, near starvation occurred on both sides. Salt pork, dried beans, hardtack, and, occasionally, coffee, were the soldier's rations when out on campaign. These troops are receiving breakfast coffee in camp.

A March in Foul Weather

The young recruit soon became accustomed to constant drill. This served him well, for a great part of the soldier's life was spent marching. Marches were undertaken in all weather at all times of the year, sometimes over great distances.

One veteran of the war remembered marching asleep on his feet through many a night, only waking at dawn, when his comrades in the ranks, having slept themselves while marching, began to waken and talk to each other.

Initiation Into Combat

The pleasures of camp life gave way to the necessities of war, as the men finished their training, were assigned to regiments, and moved out to face the enemy. Here we see the young ex-trainees, now on their way to becoming veterans, detailed to defend the artillery under fire. It was their first experience of combat.

A Meal Before Picket Duty

Soldiers in the field were regularly detailed to do picket duty—far out on the picket line in advance of the main army, they set up camp and took turns alternately watching out for enemy activity on their front, sleeping, and trying to keep warm. This picket is cooking a bit of salt pork and warming his coffee, ready to take his turn on guard.

Tension on the Firing Line

Young soldiers are pictured being sent to the firing line to defend a position where a major battle is taking place. Every man knows he might not come out alive or without serious injury. The young volunteers of yesterday are becoming veteran soldiers.

The Enemy Advances

The picket guards see an enemy skirmish line advancing upon them. It is moving ahead of the main enemy force, which can be seen raising dust on the horizon in the line of battle. The pickets will open fire and then run back to their own main line, to join their comrades in repelling the developing attack.

Making Every Vote Count

For the presidential elections of 1864, the Union army strove to make sure that every soldier's vote would count by setting up the same voting system used in the country as a whole. Voting booths, such as the tents pictured above, were set up, and the recording of votes was carried on even in the field, as we see here.

Infantry on the Attack

Infantry attacks were filled with excitement, rage, and terror. The rifled muskets, explosive shells, and canister shot used by both armies were murderous in their effect; casualty lists reflected the efficiency of these weapons. Casualties of killed, wounded, and missing were greater during the Civil War than for any other military involvement in American history.

Cavalry and Infantry Engaged in Battle

An attack by cavalry upon an infantry position was a frightening experience, and many a man who had fought bravely upon other occasions broke ranks and ran when the galloping horses and screaming, sword-swinging riders descended upon him. Some who ran away out of panic returned to the ranks later; others deserted and were not seen again by their comrades.

A Sharpshooter Takes Aim

Here we see a sharpshooter at work. Called a sniper in later wars, this accurate marksman sometimes used a specially made rifle fitted with a telescopic sight. This sharpshooter is armed with a standard Springfield infantry rifled musket fitted with such a sight. He has crept out to a secluded elevation between the lines to do his deadly work.

Helping the Wounded

In the heat of battle, a soldier helps a wounded comrade from the field to a dressing station. This was a practice often forbidden for fear that men would evade their duty in the fighting line to help a wounded man to safety in the rear, but human compassion often overruled such orders, especially when a close friend was hit.

An Army Surgeon at Work

Pictured here is an army surgeon at work at a front-line dressing station. Any man wounded in the arms or legs usually underwent amputation. The fear of death from infection was so great that only minor flesh wounds were treated in any other way than the removal of the limb. Such operations were usually conducted without anesthetics, the patient perhaps being given a drink of whiskey before the cutting began. Several men were needed to hold the victim in place so that the surgeon could use his bone saw. Death from shock, infection, and other complications was common.

Black Soldiers Join the Union Ranks

At the outbreak of the war the U.S. government decided it had no need of black soldiers, but in 1862, when casualties, disease, and desertion had thinned the ranks of blue uniforms, a Congressional act authorized their recruitment. The African-American volunteer soldier received only half the pay of the white soldier, an inequity that was not corrected until 1864. Black soldiers were given mostly hard labor jobs, but those who got into combat distinguished themselves in a number of hard-fought battles.

A Task for the Youngest Soldier

When the army was on campaign, after a hard day's march, the youngest soldier in each squad usually had the task of filling the men's canteens at the nearest creek or river. Here we see a young sol-dier transporting his comrades' canteens, which were much more burdensome to carry after they had been filled.

Fashioning a Winter Camp

In summer camp the soldiers slept in canvas tents, but for winter quarters some built crude huts, putting down a floor of split logs, fashioning bunks with bark and pine needle mattresses, and securing canvas roofs. Crude fireplaces were built for warmth. Upon returning to the war, the soldiers recalled their snug winter quarters. On campaign the men lived two to a tiny tent or improvised shelter from branches and underbrush. Possessions that could not be stuffed into a knapsack were left behind in camp.

Collecting Wages from the Paymaster

A private in the Union army received $13 a month in wages, a Confederate private, $11. When enlistment declined, bonuses were offered by the Federal and state governments. Young soldiers soon learned, however, that army pay was not as regular as had been promised. Some men were not paid for months on end. Here we see a pay line in the camp of a lucky regiment whose paymaster arrived in time for payday.

Waiting to Join the Fight

Pictured here are the soldiers of a regiment that has just arrived after a long march at the beginning of a fight. They await orders to lay down their knapsacks and move down into the field, where they will be assigned a position in the line of battle.

Behind a Defensive Line

Once deployed as part of the battle line, the men hastily threw up what defensive breastworks (a temporary fort) they could, composed perhaps of tree limbs, fence posts and rails, railroad ties—whatever they could find to provide protection from enemy bullets and shells. They then waited to defend their position against attack or to receive orders to advance. For some soldiers, waiting was the cruelest time.

Searching the Battlefield

After the battle, usually in the evening, the field was visited by soldiers detailed to carry the wounded to the dressing station; others searched the battlefield for the bodies of friends. Some came out to gather up discarded weapons and cartridge boxes, and some to take what they could from the dead and defenseless. The next day the burial parties would begin their work.

Letters from Home

A letter from a soldier's loved ones was a welcome relief from the trials of war, doubly welcome if it arrived after a battle. Reading the lines, a soldier was transported for a moment from the dreadful realities of the present to scenes of loved ones, home, and childhood.

A Forager with His Finds

As the war went on, the areas over which the fighting took place were stripped of anything edible—for men and horses—by both armies. In each regiment there always seemed to be a few men who were expert foragers. They were able to find welcome tidbits to supplement the company rations, despite severe penalties against raiding the fields and barnyards of neighboring farmers. We see a successful forager here, laden with forbidden treasures.

Mourning the Fallen

After battle the army moved on to other fields and other battles. Many a man lucky enough to march away a survivor mourned a comrade who had not survived. Here we see a soldier remembering for a moment a fallen friend. Many burial mounds were numbered; some were not marked at all.

Grand Review at War's End

When the Civil War was over (spring 1865), the U.S. War Department called for a Grand Review of the victorious Union armies in Washington, D.C. Crowds gathered to cheer as the parade marched from the U.S. capitol down Pennsylvania Avenue. After the parade, the army was broken up, regiments were sent to their native states, and men were mustered out of the service and sent home. For many who had begun as naive recruits and returned home as seasoned veterans, the war would remain the central and unforgettable event of their lives.